The Night Lion

Idea and pictures by Barbara Mossmann
Story by Werner Färber
Translated and adapted by Jane Fior

Houghton Mifflin Company

Boston 1991

It was bedtime.
Laura's mother had tucked her in and said goodnight.
Laura's father had read her a story and given her a kiss.
Neither of them had said anything about the pirates.
They hadn't even noticed them.
That was because the pirates only came out when
the bedroom light was switched off.

The minute Laura turned on the light, they disappeared.
“I know you’re there,” said Laura loudly. “Don’t think you can fool me.”
Laura knew exactly where they were hiding.
The big pirate was behind the blind.
The fat pirate was inside the puppet theater.
The nasty little one was in the dolls’ carriage.

Laura left the light on and shut her eyes tight.
Aah! What was that noise?
It must be the pirates creeping out of their
hiding places again.
Laura pulled the bedclothes over her head.
"I wish I were a lion," she said, "then I'd show them."

"Lion?" growled Otto from the toy cupboard.
"Did you call me?"
He yawned and stretched his paws.
"Otto!" said Laura. "You're awake! Do you
want to get into bed with me?"

"Yes, please," said Otto and with a bound he landed neatly on Laura's bedspread.

Otto put his paw around Laura. Now she felt snug and safe. But no sooner had she shut her eyes than she heard it again. That rustling, shuffling noise. Otto didn't hear it. He was fast asleep and snoring loudly.

"Wake up!" said Laura, giving him a shake. "You mustn't go to sleep. You've got to look after me."

"Look after you?" repeated Otto, opening his eyes wearily. "I'm far too tired."

"I'll tell you a story if you like," said Laura.
"Can it be about a big strong lion?" asked Otto, showing more interest.
"I don't know one about a lion," said Laura. "What about this one? Once upon a time there was a fierce green dragon . . ."
"Stop!" shrieked Otto, covering his ears. "Don't tell me any more. It's too scary."

"That's a shame," said Laura. "I really like that story. I can't think of another one. Let's play hide-and-seek instead."
"I'll only play if I can hide first," said Otto.
"All right," said Laura, "but you've got to promise to stay awake and look after me."
She turned around, shut her eyes and began to count.
"One. Two. Three – Coming!"
"Otto," scolded Laura, "you've gone to sleep *again*. Wake up! You mustn't go to sleep."

"But I'm so tired," complained Otto.
"Otto, please try and stay awake. Would you like to play Catch?"
"That," said Otto, "would make me even tireder."
Laura tugged his tail. "Then we'll play something else, but you've got to join in."

Laura tipped everything out of the dressing-up box.
"Choose something to put on, then I'll guess what you are and you can guess what I am."
"Ready?" asked Laura.
"Ready," said Otto.
"Then turn around," said Laura.

“I know what you are,” said Laura. “Can I have first guess?”
Otto nodded.
“You’re a –– witch!”
Otto shook his head. “No, I’m not,” he said.
“I’m a pirate.”

"That's not fair, Otto," said Laura. "You know
I'm scared of pirates."
"Why?" said Otto. "I'm a very friendly pirate."
"It doesn't make any difference. I still don't like pirates.
Now it's your turn to guess."
"You're a –– crocodile!" said Otto.
"No," said Laura.

"I'm a great big fierce green dragon!"

With a shriek, Otto jumped straight back on top of the cupboard.
"What's the matter?" called Laura. "Did I frighten you? I'm sorry, Otto. I didn't know you were *that* scared of dragons."
Otto didn't reply. He was too frightened to speak.
"Please come down," said Laura. "Look, I'm not really a fierce green dragon. I'll be a crocodile if you like."

Märchen

After a while, Otto clambered down.
"I'm glad you're not a dragon any more," he said.
"Otto?"
"Yes?" said Otto.
"How do you go to sleep if you're scared of dragons?"
"Well, I'm not scared if you're there," said Otto.
"But what if I go to sleep?" asked Laura.

"That doesn't matter," said Otto. "If you're asleep and a dragon comes to catch me, I'll shout out your name and you'll wake up and rescue me!" Laura yawned. "And if pirates come in the middle of the night to take me away, I'll wake *you* up."
"And I'll rescue you," said Otto. And he turned out the light.

**The next morning Laura and Otto looked at each other.
They had both slept soundly all night long.**

First American edition 1991
Originally published in Germany in 1989 by Verlag Herder Freiburg
im Breisgau

Printed in Great Britain by
Cambus Litho, Great Britain.

10 9 8 7 6 5 4 3 2 1

ISBN 0-395-57816-7

CIP information is available from the U.S. Library of Congress.